CAP
JENNIFER
JELLYFISH JONES

by
VIVIAN FRENCH

Illustrated by
CHRIS FISHER

*Hodder
Children's
Books*

a division of Hodder Headline plc

For Nicola with love
Vivian French

To Glenn, Sam, Mo and Ben with love
Chris Fisher

Text copyright © 1995 Vivian French
Illustrations copyright © Chris Fisher

First published in Great Britain in 1995
by Hodder Children's Books

10 9 8 7 6 5 4 3 2 1

A Catalogue record for this book is available from the British Library

ISBN 0340 619503

Printed and bound in Great Britain by
Cox & Wyman Ltd, Reading, Berks.

Hodder Children's Books
A Division of Hodder Headline plc
338 Euston Road
London NW1 3BH

CHAPTER ONE

When Jennifer Jones was born the first thing she did was decide to be a pirate. When she was one she asked for a black patch to cover one eye, and when she was two she asked for a cutlass. By the time she was six she had two pairs of huge sea boots, a hat with a skull and crossbones on it and a spotty hankie to tie round her neck.

On her seventh birthday she had a disappointment.

"What's this?" she asked her mum.

"It's a chicken," said her mum.

"But I wanted a parrot called Polly," said Jenny.

"Too expensive," said her mum crisply.

Jenny scratched her head and looked at the chicken.

"Cluck," it clucked, and fluttered its eyelashes. Jenny sighed. "O.K.," she said, "but you'll have to learn to sit on my shoulder. And you'll have to learn fast. I want to go to sea next Tuesday."

"CLUCK!" said Polly.

When Tuesday came Jennifer Jones put on her hat and her sea boots and tied her spotty hankie round her neck.

"Shiver my timbers and off I go to sea," she said.

"Just a moment," said her mum. "WHERE did you say you were going?"

"To sea," Jenny said.

"Cluck!" said Polly.

Jenny's mum looked doubtful. "Hum. You're a little young to go on your own." She thought for a moment. "I know! You can take Roger from next door with you."

Jenny groaned. "MUST I? Roger's so miserable."

"Yes." Her mum nodded her head. "Roger is old enough to be sensible. He babysits for Mrs Moore's Bobby.

Besides, the fresh air might cheer him up."

Jenny groaned again and went to collect Roger.

Roger opened the door. He looked miserable as usual.

"Hello," said Jenny. "I'm going to be a pirate, and my mum says you're to come too."

"Oh." Roger looked even more miserable. "I charge one pound fifty an hour for baby sitting."

"But I'm not a baby," Jenny said. "You'll be paid in gold and diamonds and rubies and pieces of eight. I'm going to be a Pirate Captain."

"Well..." Roger leant against the door frame. "Um. If I came with you I wouldn't have to babysit for Mrs Moore, would I?"

Jenny shook her head.

"And you haven't got any babies going with you?"

Jenny shook her head again.

Roger suddenly looked almost cheerful. "I never did like babies. I'll go and pack."

"Good," Jenny said. "I'll lend you my spare pair of sea boots to wear."

7

Jenny went back to her own house with Roger.

"Here we are, Mum," she said. "Spit in my eye and we're off to make our fortune on the high seas."

Mrs Jones sighed. "I've made you some sandwiches," she said. "And don't forget to send a postcard. And I won't spit in your eye just now, thank you all the same."

"Thanks, Mum," said Jenny, and

she swaggered quickly out of the house before her mum thought of anything else. Polly swayed on Jenny's shoulder, and Roger clumped along behind her.

Jennifer Jones banged the garden gate behind them.

"Shopping first," she said, and swung her cutlass round her head. Polly let out a terrified cluck and ducked.

"Sorry, Polly," said Jenny. "Step lively, Roger. We're off to Pegleg Pete's."

"O.K.," said Roger. "I mean, yes, Captain Jenny."

Jenny stared at him. "Try, 'AYE AYE CAP'N!'"

Roger coughed. "Ahem. Aye aye, Captain!"

CHAPTER TWO

Pegleg Pete's Pirate Emporium was on the edge of the harbour.

"And what can I do for you, young lady and gent?" Pegleg asked. "We don't be selling sweeties and lollies in this 'ere shop, nor dollies neither."

Jenny jumped onto a barrel, and swished her cutlass so close to Pegleg's nose that his eyes popped.

"First," said Jenny, "I want a ship.

Then, I want a crew – the wildest and wickedest crew you've got – and then I want the longest, strongest gangplank in this mouldy old shop. AND I" – she swished her cutlass the other way – "am NOT a young lady."

Pegleg Pete nodded his head so hard his hat fell off. "I can see that, kind miss ... er, sir ... er ... Who might I 'ave the 'onour to be talking to?"

Jennifer Jones opened her mouth and then stopped. High up on Pegleg Pete's wall was a picture of a ferocious jellyfish swirling through the waves. Jenny folded her arms and glared.

"I am Captain Jennifer Jellyfish Jones," she announced. "And anyone who gets in my way shakes like a JELLY before I feed 'em to the FISH. GET IT?"

GRRR!!

11

"Oh yes, indeed – and a real 'onour it is to serve you, Cap'n Jellyfish." Pegleg nodded and bowed, and hurried away into the darkness at the back of the shop.

Roger was bending over a large box. It was howling loudly and jumping about.

"What's that" Jenny asked.

"It's a dog, Captain," Roger said. "It appears to be called Williams. I expect it bites."

"H'm. I hadn't thought of a dog, but I'm sure we ought to have one," Jenny said. "How old is it?"

"I don't know," Roger said. "Why?"

"Every pirate ship has an old sea dog on board," Jenny told him. "Let's take him with us."

Sea Dog Williams barked in wild enthusiasm, fell out of the box and hurled himself at Jenny and Roger.

Pegleg Pete came hurrying out from the back of the shop dragging a gangplank behind him. "Will you be taking the crew now, sir and Cap'n? Or would you prefer as I have them delivered straight down to the Ghastly Ghoul – she's the bestest ship as I've got." He gave Sea Dog Williams a quick glare. "And I'll throw that there animal in fer free, kind sirs."

Jenny stepped forward. "So I should hope," she said. "And we'll take the crew and supplies now, and hurry up about it." She swished her cutlass, and Pegleg Pete scuttled out to his store cupboard.

When Jenny saw the crew she wondered how on earth she was going to lead them down to the ship.

Roger shuddered and went
pale. Sea Dog Williams began
to whine and tried to sit
on Jenny's lap.

"CLUCK!" said Polly.

They were the wildest, wickedest
looking pirates ever seen, and they
were snarling and growling and
spitting as they came rolling out
carrying the boxes and bags
and barrels of food and
drink for the
voyage.

GRRRR

"Look 'em over, Cap'n," said Pegleg Pete, rubbing his hands together. "These is the best quality supplies and the evilest hearted crew as ever you'll see."

"Er ... very nice," said Jenny. Roger nodded. "Splendid, in fact," said Jenny. Roger nodded again.

A small foxy faced pirate sneered.

Captain Jennifer Jellyfish Jones suddenly remembered who she was. She sprang onto the wooden counter and stamped her foot and whirled her cutlass round her head.

"You horrible swabs!" she shouted. "Get into line and get marching down to the Ghastly Ghoul. And don't even THINK of a growl or a snarl against me, your Captain – or you'll find out just WHY I'm called Captain Jellyfish Jones!"

The pirates shivered and hurried into a straggly line. Then they slunk out of the door, and Captain Jenny strutted behind them.

"Er ... excuse me for the mentioning of it, kind sirs," said Pegleg as Roger and Sea Dog Williams hurried after Jenny with the gangplank, "but was you thinking of paying?"

Jenny froze him with a look.

"We'll pay you when we've tried out the goods," she said. "IF the ship and crew are what we expect them to be we'll pay you on return. If not – we'll be back to chop you up into teensy weensy little pieces."

And the shop door slammed shut.

CHAPTER THREE

The Ghastly Ghoul was tied up to the harbour wall. She was painted black all over, and her black sails flapped gloomily in the wind. Even the mooring rope was black, and sharp nosed black rats ran up and down it. Instead of a figurehead a huge black skull stared out across the waves, and only its teeth were gleaming white.

Jenny took hold of one end of the gangplank and winked at Roger. Together they heaved it towards the crew.

"CATCH!" shouted Captain Jellyfish Jones as the crew dropped the heavy plank on their toes.

"Ho ho ho!" said Roger. Jenny looked at him in surprise, and he blushed. "I thought it was time for a bloodthirsty laugh. I don't suppose it was very good."

"It wasn't bad," Jenny said approvingly. She turned and glared at the pirates.

"Get on board! We set sail at sundown!" The crew limped up the gangplank and on to the deck of the Ghastly Ghoul.

At sundown, nothing was ready. All the pirates were so wild and wicked that they kept fighting each other instead of getting on with the job of heaving on ropes and pulling up the sails. Jenny swished her cutlass and shouted at them, but as soon as one group began to work another group began to fight.

"Bother," said Jenny. "Jolly Roger and Sea Dog Williams, I think we need a parley."

"A what?" said Roger.

"Woof?" said Williams.

"A chat," said Jenny. They all stamped down to the captain's cabin.

"Cluck," clucked Polly.

In the cabin Jenny shared out her mum's sandwiches, while up above the thumpings and bashings went on.

"So what are we going to do?" she asked. "If we don't stop them fighting we'll NEVER get to sea. And I don't think much of being a Pirate captain who never leaves the shore."

"If I were you," said a voice, "I'd just let them all get on with it."

"WHAT?????????" Jenny and Roger stared.

"CLUCK?" said Polly.

Sea Dog Williams hid under the table.

There was a creaking noise, and the portrait of a whiskery pirate swung to one side. Behind it was a dark space, and a small round boy grinning at them.

"Hi!" he said.

Jenny stood up and bowed. "Captain Jennifer Jellyfish Jones," she said. "Captain of the Ghastly Ghoul, and all who sail in her. And this is Roger, and that is Sea Dog Williams."

The boy stepped into the cabin. "First Mate Mutt," he said, "at your service."

"Excuse me mentioning it," said Jenny, "but aren't you a very YOUNG first mate?"

Mutt looked at her. "Aren't you a very young captain?"

"I've been a pirate for AGES," Jenny said. "I decided to be a pirate when I was born."

"Well," said Mutt, "I've been a pirate for ages too. I was cook's boy for a while and then cabin boy for a couple of voyages, but I got bored.

That's why I decided to be First Mate."

"Oh," Jenny said. "I don't think that's the way it's usually done."

Mutt sighed. "I know. I've been thinking of going on shore and being an inventor instead."

Roger was peering into the space behind the picture. "Is this a secret passage?" he asked.

Mutt nodded. "Yes. I've built them all over the ship. This old hulk's been lying here for MONTHS."

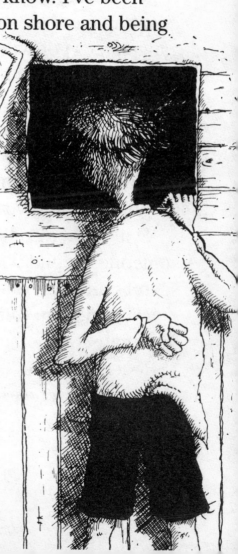

Jenny frowned. "But Pegleg Pete said this was his BEST ship!"

Mutt shrugged. "It's his ONLY ship. Pegleg was a pirate so you have to expect him to be a wicked, wily, cheating liar. I expect your gangplank's got woodworm and your biscuits are full of beetles."

Jenny was thoughtful. It seemed there were still things she needed to know about the world of pirates. It could be useful to have someone around who knew what was what. AND it could also be useful to have someone around who could build secret passages. She looked at Roger.

"What do you think? Do we need a first mate?"

Roger coughed. "Are YOU a wicked, wily, cheating liar?" he asked Mutt sternly.

Mutt grinned. "No," he said. "But if I was I'd still say I wasn't. So you'll have to find out."

Jenny laughed. "O.K.," she said. "You can be our First Mate."

Mutt shook hands with Jenny and Roger. Then he shook Sea Dog Williams' paw and stroked Polly's feathers.

"Hurrah for Captain Jennifer Jellyfish Jones!" he said.

"Hurrah! for the team that sail with her!" said Jenny.

"WOOF!" said Sea Dog Williams.

"CLUCK!" said Polly.

27

There was a staggering

from the deck above. Williams
scuttled back under the table.

"Oh dear," said Jenny. "We ought
to do something about the crew."

"Nothing you can do," said Mutt.
"Leave them 'til the morning."

Jenny yawned. "Fair enough.
Who's on cocoa duty?"

Roger stood up. "I used to make
cocoa sometimes when I was
babysitting."

In only five minutes they
were drinking
large mugs of
thick sugary
cocoa.

"Well done, Roger," Jenny said. "And now it's time to turn in."

Williams leapt onto the end of Jenny's bunk. Mutt slapped Roger on the back.

"You can share my cabin," he said. "Although it may be a bit noisy."

Roger sighed heavily. "I don't expect any of us will get any sleep at all," he said. "And there'll probably be a storm tomorrow."

"Probably," said Mutt, and he winked at Jenny. Jenny winked back.

"Do you think it'll be a terribly BAD storm?" she asked Roger, looking very serious. Roger nodded. "Sure to be, Captain."

29

Jenny began to laugh, but managed to turn it into a cough before Roger noticed. A sudden idea struck her. "Hey!" she said. "I've just thought! You need a proper piratical name – what about JOLLY Roger?"

Roger looked surprised. "Oh," he said. "My mum always says I'm not a jolly person at all. Still, you're the captain." He sighed again. "As long as we don't have a mutiny. Or a riot. Or all get eaten by sharks – "

"GOOD NIGHT, Jolly Roger!" Jenny said firmly. "Take him away, First Mate Mutt!"

Mutt snorted, and pushed Roger towards the secret passage. "Come and see my invention for boiling an egg while you're lying in your hammock," he said. "It's one of my best ever. I just wish I had an egg."

Captain Jennifer Jellyfish Jones waved as Roger and Mutt disappeared. Then she cleaned her teeth and hopped into her bunk. Above her the whackings and thumpings were still going on, but the moment she closed her eyes she went straight to sleep.

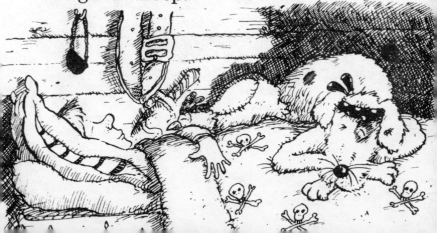

CHAPTER FOUR

When morning came it was very, very quiet. A few seagulls were shrieking, but there was no sound at all from the pirates. Jenny, Roger, Mutt and Williams tiptoed out of their cabins and up on deck.

"WELL!" Jenny said as she stared round. All the pirates were there, but they were lying in heaps and not moving so much as an eye patch.

"They've knocked each other out," said Mutt.

"But I want to get to sea TODAY," Jenny said.

They all looked at the silent heaps of pirates.

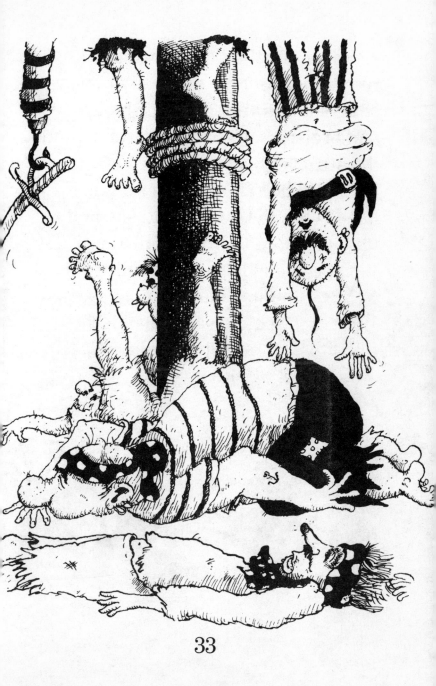

Roger coughed. "It's probably a rotten idea, but my mum always says cold water is very good for bumps and bruises." He coughed again. "And the sea's very cold..."

"BRILLIANT!" said Jenny. "All hands OFF the deck!" And she and Mutt and Roger pulled up their sleeves and rolled the pirates into the cold green sea. As each one hit the water they woke up with a yell.

At the end of ten minutes they were all hanging on to the anchor chain and begging for help.

"Cap'n! Dear, kind, wonderful cap'n...we be WET!"

(Loud splashings)

"Do 'ee be letting us come back on board!?"

(More splashings)

"There's none of us can swim!"

("CAN'T US?"

"No – we ain't got our water wings")

"HELPPPPPPPPPPP!!!!!!!!!"

(VERY loud splashings)

"Cap'n! If we drowns here so close to land we'll be laughed at by all the pirate fleets!"

"We'll do ANYFING, Cap'n – just haul us up!"

Captain Jenny, First Mate Mutt and Jolly Roger folded their arms and glared down. Sea Dog Williams growled loudly.

"We'll haul you up," Jenny growled, "but only if you PROMISE to behave."

"Oh yes, yes, yes, we'll PROMISE," the pirates snivelled.

Jolly Roger noticed the small foxy faced pirate winking at the others in a plotting sort of way.

"Let's hear you swear on the skull of the Ghastly Ghoul," he snapped.

"And NO crossed fingers behind your backs!" added Mutt.

"That's right," said Jenny.
"And the first to break their promise
will be fed to the jellyfish in eighty
four separate pieces."

"WOOF!" barked Sea Dog Williams.

Polly didn't say anything. Sea Dog
Williams nudged her.

"CLUCK!"

There was a shifty silence from
the waves below, and then some
muttering.

"Wot d'yer fink, Foxy Ratt?"

"Wot d'we do, Foxy?"

"Foxy, me teeth is chattering!
Get us out!"

37

The foxy faced pirate growled and spat. In a sulky voice he said, "We swear, Cap'n."

"Good!" said Jenny, and Mutt and Roger wound up the anchor chain so fast that the wild and wicked pirates had to leap for their lives as they reached the deck.

"Now – jump to it!" shouted Jenny, and they did.

The Ghastly Ghoul sailed away at six o'clock that evening. Her black sails billowed out in the westerly wind, and the skull and crossbones fluttered on the mast. Captain Jenny Jellyfish Jones stood proudly watching as the land slipped away behind her.

"A pirate's life is a wonderful life," she said to Jolly Roger and First Mate Mutt, and she twirled in her sea boots and waved her cutlass in the air. "And now we can look for treasure! Rubies and diamonds and pieces of eight!"

"Something'll probably go wrong tomorrow," Roger said, but he didn't look at all miserable as he said it.

Mutt pulled a tangled collection of wires from his pocket. "If only I had an egg I could try out my invention. Then life on the Ghastly Ghoul would be just perfect."

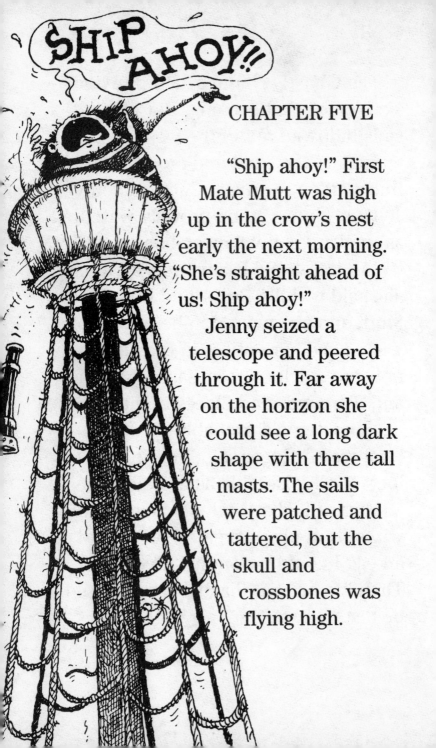

CHAPTER FIVE

"Ship ahoy!" First Mate Mutt was high up in the crow's nest early the next morning. "She's straight ahead of us! Ship ahoy!"

Jenny seized a telescope and peered through it. Far away on the horizon she could see a long dark shape with three tall masts. The sails were patched and tattered, but the skull and crossbones was flying high.

"We'll capture her!" Jenny shouted.
"Steer straight towards her!"

There was a muttering and a scowling from all around.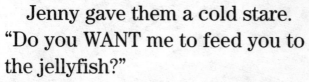

"We be tired, Cap'n."

"'Tis hard work, all this sailing."

"'Tis too soon to be fighting and bashing all over again"

Jenny gave them a cold stare. "Do you WANT me to feed you to the jellyfish?"

The crew shuffled about.

"We're going to capture that ship," Jenny said, "and THEN there'll be a reward for EVERYONE."

Foxy Ratt sneered. "How do 'ee know as there's anything on board that there poxy ship, Cap'n?"

41

He swung a large wooden hammer perilously near Jenny's toes.

"Yeah!" Several other pirates bristled their beards at Jenny and bunched together in a menacing way. "Foxy's right!"

Up in the crow's nest First Mate Mutt looked down. "Aha!" he said.

A gaping hole appeared in the deck and the bunch of pirates disappeared into it. Muffled shouts and curses floated up as one by one the pirates landed on the ship's cook.

Captain Jenny Jellyfish Jones tried not to look startled. Foxy Ratt backed away hurriedly dropping his hammer into the water barrel, while his eyes popped out of his head.

"Er...beg pardin, Cap'n," he said. "Just as you say. We'll set course right now."

"And so I should hope." Jenny put her hands on her hips and swaggered. "And just remember that you never know *what* I might do!"

And she strutted away to her cabin where she found Jolly Roger trying to teach Sea Dog Williams and Polly to play cards.

"That was a near thing!" Jenny said. "Three cheers for First Mate Mutt!"

Mutt popped his head out from behind the pirate portrait.

"Did you call?"

Jenny shook her head. "You're amazing."

"I know," said Mutt, and vanished again.

CHAPTER SIX

CAPTAIN! CAPTAIN!!

"That's Mutt!" Jenny,
Roger, Polly and Williams rushed up
on deck, Jenny buckling on her
cutlass as she went. The Ghastly
Ghoul, with First Mate Mutt at the
wheel, was close behind the other
ship and catching up fast.

"We're coming up alongside, Cap'n,"
said Mutt. "It's the Wicked Winnie –
we'll have her captured in no time."

45

Jenny whipped out her telescope and peered at the Winnie. Her crew were frantically paddling with brushes, buckets and planks of wood – anything to make her go faster. They were staring over their shoulders at the Ghoul, and the closer she came the faster they paddled.

GULP!

"They look terrified," Jenny said.

Mutt grinned. "They've seen our crew," he said, and pointed. Jenny looked up. All her pirates were sitting in the rigging pulling terrible faces at the Wicked Winnie. Sea Dog Williams shuddered. Polly shivered

"GRRRRRRRRRR!!!!"

inside her feathers.

"WOW!" said Roger.

"Well done, First Mate Mutt!" said
Jenny. She swung her cutlass in the
air. "GET READY TO BOARD!"

There was a flurry of activity.
The Ghastly Ghoul's crew tumbled
down onto the deck, slapping each
other on the back.

"Proper scaredy cats, they be!"

The grappling irons were
hauled out.

"We've got 'em licked already!"

The iron hooks were heaved over the side of the Winnie. The Winnie's crew dropped everything and dashed below decks.

"Running away to hide, they is!"

Soon the Winnie was lashed firmly alongside.

"They'll be beggin' us for mercy as we shivers their timbers!"

"NOW LISTEN!" Jenny stamped her foot. First Mate Mutt blew a piercingly loud whistle. The crew froze.

The crew of the Ghastly Ghoul went pale. They opened their mouths to revolt, but Captain Jennifer Jellyfish Jones leapt in the air.

"ACTION!" she yelled, and leapt over the side of the Ghoul and onto the the Wicked Winnie.

"HURRAH FOR THE GHASTLY GHOUL!" shouted First Mate Mutt and tumbled after her, closely followed by Jolly Roger and Sea Dog Williams. Polly flew above them clucking loudly. The pirates, caught up in the rush, scrambled behind.

At exactly that moment the Wicked Winnie's crew came surging back onto the deck. They were green with fright, but they wore a look of grim determination and they were armed to the teeth with cutlasses, swords and daggers.

"EEEEEEEEEEEEEEEEK!"

The Ghastly Ghoul pirates stopped dead.

"Thought you said as they was scaredy cats, Foxy," said an anxious voice.

"Er..." said Foxy.

"JELLYFISH FOR EVER!" shrieked Captain Jennifer Jellyfish Jones. She dashed at the largest and fiercest looking Wicked Winnie pirate and bopped him on the head with the handle of her cutlass. He let out a loud howl and fell over.

"MUTT! MUTT! MUTT!" screeched Mutt, and bopped another.

"YAH! BOO! And DOWN you go!"
Jolly Roger biffed a third.

"GRRRRRRRRRRRRRR!" growled
Williams, and downed a fourth.

"CLUCKKKKKKKKK!"
clucked Polly. A fifth
pirate took a swing at her,
missed, and flattened
three others.

"WELL DONE, POLLY!"
Captain Jennifer Jellyfish Jones
cheered as she whirled her cutlass
round and round her head.

The Wicked Winnie pirates
hesitated. One dropped his sword.
Another held up a dirty white
hankie. Foxy Ratt seized his
moment.

"Here we come, Cap'n!"
And the crew of the Ghastly Ghoul
threw themselves into the fight.

51

"STOPPPPPPPPPPPPP!"

Captain Jenny signalled to Mutt, and Mutt blew on his whistle.

"We can't stop now, Cap'n!" Foxy Ratt was furious.

"Oh yes we can," said Captain Jennifer.

It was all over in minutes. The Wicked Winnie crew gave in, and Sea Dog Williams lined them up in sniffling, snivelling rows. The crew of the Ghastly Ghoul stood behind them scowling and glaring and muttering darkly.

"EASY PEASY! What a load of softies!"

"Can't we shiver even ONE timber?"

"PRISONERS! Give us some guts for garters!"

"YEAH!"

"Piffling soppy girls! You'll have
to do 'er in, Foxy!"

Foxy Ratt tapped the side of his
nose. "Just you wait, me hearties!"
he hissed. "It'll be mutiny yet!"

CHAPTER SEVEN

Captain Jenny Jellyfish Jones,
First Mate Mutt, Jolly Roger and Sea
Dog Williams marched slowly up and
down inspecting their prisoners.

"H'mph!" said Jenny. "A pretty
poor lot!"

"Hang 'em from the yard arm,
Cap'n!" Foxy Ratt shouted.

Jenny shook her head. "No,"
she said. "Any prisoners that
want to can walk the plank
and take their chance. I don't
THINK there are any sharks
about. And we'll let them
have the Wicked Winnie to
swim to IF they can swim.
But any crew that want to
stay here on board the
Ghastly Ghoul can."

Foxy Ratt snarled softly, and moved close to the water barrel. Several other pirates snorted angrily. The rest brightened. It was always fun watching people walk the plank.

Jolly Roger and First Mate Mutt organised the plank. One small Wicked Winnie crew member stepped forward, looking nervously at Sea Dog Williams. He limped down the plank and splashed into the sea.

The crew of the Ghastly Ghoul cheered in a half-hearted way.

"He should be tied up," Foxy grumbled. "And there should be 'orrible beastly sharkses waiting to bite off his toeses!"

"RIGHT! Anyone else?" Jenny wanted to know. The remaining prisoners shook their heads. The Wicked Winnie was damp, smelly and uncomfortable.

"Let go the Wicked Winnie!" Jenny commanded.

As the Winnie drifted away the wild and wicked pirates of the Ghastly Ghoul looked furtively at Foxy Ratt.

"Come on, Foxy!"

"Wild and wicked, we is!"

"It just ain't done!" said Foxy, and he reached down into the water

barrel for the big wooden hammer.
"We be pirates, not sissy soppy
girlies." And slowly,
silently, he edged his
way towards Jenny.
Sniffy Smith and Long Jon
Mustard sneaked and slid
their way behind Jolly
Roger at the ship's wheel.
Toothy and several others
crept round the mast and
behind First Mate Mutt.

Foxy Ratt's beady little
eyes were swivelling this
way and that. He saw the
other pirates sneaking
into position, and he
grinned his foxy grin. All
at once he sprang at
Captain Jennifer Jellyfish
Jones.

"GRRRRRRRRR!"

At exactly the same moment Sea Dog Williams grabbed Foxy's ankle in his teeth. Foxy fell flat on his face.

GRRRRRR!

YEEEEEEOWW!!

Everybody except for Captain Jennifer Jellyfish Jones jumped.

"WHAT?"

"MUTINY?"

"No, no, First Mate Mutt, sir – "

"We was just looking at the view – "

"Very pretty it is, sir, very pretty – "

"WOOF!"

"What were YOU doing, Sniffy?"

"We was coming to help steer – honest we was!"

"CLUCK!"

"AVAST THERE, ME HEARTIES!" Captain Jennifer Jellyfish Jones stood tall on the top of a barrel and took no notice of the flustered mutterings all around her. Sniffy, Long Jon and Toothy stood up straight and smiled bright we–didn't–do–nothing–COR–how–could–you–have–thought–it smiles. The other pirates tried hard not to look shifty. Foxy tried to breathe under the weight of Sea Dog Williams.

GRRRR

NICE DOGGY GULP!

"Well done, my pirates!" shouted
Captain Jennifer. "We captured the
Wicked Winnie, and now you shall
have your reward!"

There was total silence. The pirates
from both ships were staring at her
with their mouths wide open.

First Mate Mutt grinned at Roger,
and Roger winked back.

"You see," Jenny went on, "you did
as you were told. You are all wild and
wicked, and it isn't easy for you – so

the prisoners from the Wicked Winnie
will give you your reward. They will
stay on board the Ghastly Ghoul for
two weeks and they will clean and
cook and sail the ship... and my crew
will have a holiday!"

The silence went on. Then –

The cheers could be heard from three miles away. The crew of the Ghastly Ghoul cheered until they were hoarse, and then cheered again in whispers.

Foxy Ratt wasn't cheering. Sea Dog Williams was growling in his ear, while Polly scuttled about pushing a large wooden hammer under a pile of rope. Only First Mate Mutt and Jolly Roger saw what she was doing. They also saw Foxy slinking away into the bilges to hide...

First Mate Mutt, Jolly Roger and Sea Dog Williams shook hands and paws, and then marched off with Captain Jenny to enjoy a truly splendiferous supper cooked by the crew of the Wicked Winnie.

"Three cheers for the Ghastly Ghoul!" said Jolly Roger.

"A pirate's life is a wonderful life!" said Jenny. "And NOW we can get on with looking for treasure! Rubies and diamonds and pieces of eight!"

"Very nearly perfect," said First Mate Mutt with his mouth full. He pulled his egg boiling machine out of his pocket and looked at it wistfully. "But not QUITE perfect."

"Woof!" said Sea Dog Williams.

"Cluck!" said Polly, and laid an egg.